Babar characters TM & © 1990 L. de Brunhoff
All rights reserved.
Based on the animated series "Babar"
A Nelvana-Ellipse Presentation
a Nelvana Production in Association with The Clifford Ross Company, Ltd

Based on characters created
by Jean and Laurent de Brunhoff

Image adaptation by Van Gool-Lefevre-Loiseaux
Produced by Twin Books U.K. Ltd, London

This 1990 edition published by JellyBean Press,
distributed by Outlet Book Company, Inc.,
A Random House Company, 225 Park Avenue South,
New York, New York 10003

ISBN 0-517-05209-1

8 7 6 5 4 3 2 1
Printed in Italy

BABAR™

and His Friends

At the Amusement Park

Twin Books

JellyBean Press
New York

Today, a rippling  of blue and gold is

flying in the park. The carnival has come to town!

A  arrives, soon followed by an old-

fashioned wagon rather like a gypsy  .

Through the streets of Celesteville, a canopied car

equipped with a  spreads the word:

"Come to the carnival, everyone! There will be

games, rides, food, and fireworks!"

A delightful  is set up in the middle

of the park. Everyone works hard to get things

ready for the great day.

flag, trailer, caravan, loudspeaker, merry-go-round

In a big shed, the children are secretly building

a tremendous float for the carnival's parade.

"Our  is really good," says Flora,

stepping back to admire their progress. She

has on a , her costume as a ballerina.

"Alexander," says Arthur, who is directing them,

"please go faster with your ! And get a

new  of black paint for the dragon's claws."

Pom is cutting up lots and lots of colored paper

with their  to make a paper chain for

the float. "Let's not waste any time," he says.

dragon, tutu,
paintbrush, can,
scissors

The big parade has just reached the palace grounds.

"I hear a loud ," says Babar to Celeste.

"Look at the majorettes!" she replies. "How well they

march along together and twirl the  !

They look very smart in their bright uniforms and

white . What a delightful parade!"

The king of the kangaroos has joined the band,

proud of his new , with its gold braid and

visor. In honor of the king and queen, the musicians

play a loud  fanfare. "Hurry, Babar,"

says Celeste excitedly. "It's time to go."

drum, baton, boots, hat, trumpet

In the street, everyone is admiring the wonderful

float pulled by the  Gregory in harness.

"It is very well done," says Celeste admiringly.

Pom calls, "I made the big 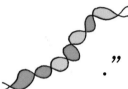 ."

"All the children are in costume," says Babar. "I

can recognize Pom in the  suit, and behind

that  on the clown is Arthur."

"I don't see Alexander anywhere," says Celeste.

At that moment, a fierce, furry little

stops in front of her, waving and making scary

faces. "That must be Alexander," sighs Celeste.

lion, paper chain,
harlequin, mask,
gorilla

The parade slows down and Pom throws

at the spectators. What a colorful sight it is!

Everyone is in the mood to celebrate. Celeste

throws out a  and thinks it's great fun.

Alexander is still pretending to be fierce, and a

child starts to cry, but not because he's scared.

"Oh, my 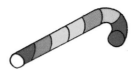 !" he wails. "I dropped it!"

"Don't worry," Babar consoles him. "Look at the

beautiful  as they float into the sky."

"Let the carnival begin!" cries Arthur. "The summer

sky is so  . Let's have a good time."

confetti,
streamer,
candycane,
balloons,
blue

The children are eager for their first ride.

Arthur hesitates between the

and the other five seats on the carousel.

"Choose one," calls Celeste. "It's about to start."

Arthur jumps into the little bus with its

that blink on and off. He's just in time! High

up in the , Alexander and Flora

pretend they are astronauts in outer space.

Pom's  doesn't really take off, as

he hoped, but he is lucky to catch the pompom.

"Next time," he says, "I'll ride the  ."

helicopter,
headlights,
flying saucer,
airplane,
motor scooter

On the merry-go-round, the Old Lady is admiring

a wooden  with a dappled coat.

"I'll help you up," offers Babar. "Steady: be

careful you don't slide off the shiny ."

"Come with me, Celeste. It will be such fun!"

Celeste chooses the  to ride in, and

Zephir is the coachman. When the merry-go-round

starts, he gives a loud crack of the .

"I feel as though I'm really off on a trip!" calls

Celeste, as she opens up her .

Poor Babar: He wasn't quick enough to get a ride!

horse, saddle, carriage, whip, parasol

By this time, the children have taken off their

costumes to walk through the amusement park.

"Mmm, it smells good! I'd like to try that  ,"

exclaims Pom. "But then maybe I'd rather have

something else, like this big 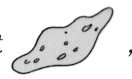 !"

"Always thinking of your stomach," laughs Alexander.

"Well, your chocolate is big enough!"

replies Pom. "And besides that, you've got a

whole bag of  as well. Want to share?"

Flora, always generous, dips into her sackful

of for a puppy that is begging.

Pom wants to eat his big  , but

Alexander pulls him along, saying, "Come on,

Papa is meeting us over at the  !"

Babar is having a grand time, especially since

Rataxes has joined him on the exciting ride.

Babar goes so fast the electric makes

sparks. BANG! He bumps into the surprised

Rataxes, who lets go of the  and yells.

"Come on, let's go ourselves," Arthur urges Zephir.

"Yes!" agrees Zephir, and he buys them each

a so that they can ride.

hot dog,
bumper car,
rod,
steering wheel,
token

"Let's go to the games of chance," suggests Flora.

"Look, the huge  is spinning!"

Arthur, Pom, and Alexander all want to play too.

The  is the prize Arthur wants most.

Flora is hoping that no one else will win the

beautiful  she sees on the first shelf.

"It's number eight–I've won!" exclaims the Old

Lady in surprise, as she looks at her .

Flora is so disappointed that the Old Lady kindly

gives her the she has won, saying,

"Really, I'd rather have won the  ."

wheel of fortune,
radio,
doll,
ticket,
goldfish,
plant

"Oh, good, the haunted house ride! Let's go!"

says Pom. "Yes," agrees Flora. "It's really fun."

Arthur helps them all get into the

and they speed into the dark tunnel. The first

thing that pops out is a ! Pom edges

over still closer to Alexander. Then he cries,

"Eeek, a red  !" He is getting quite scared.

Even Arthur is frightened when a ghost flies by

overhead, rattling a rusty metal  !

Then it's Alexander's turn to be startled. He yells,

"Yikes, a  ! It's right near my head!"

car,
skull,
devil,
chain,
bat

When they leave the haunted house, they see

Babar standing with a target

at the shooting gallery. Arthur wants to try out

the rifle, and Alexander wants the long  .

Babar concentrates and aims, when suddenly–

"I hit the !" shouts Alexander.

His yell surprises Babar, who misses his shot

at the . He's not very pleased!

But Celeste says, "Well done, Alexander," and

Babar looks at the and laughs. "What

a marksman! He's better than I am!"

rifle,
bow,
Indian,
target,
arrow

Pom, Flora, and Alexander hear the loud sound

of a hand  ringing under the big tent. "Come

in, come in" cries the barker, "and see Zouzou

the  , the cleverest one in the world!"

"All right," cries Pom, and he picks up a

with a number on it. "I'm sure that Zouzou will

go right for the  in box number eight!"

Alexander and Flora want to play the game, too.

Then the barker picks up the  , and the

little guinea pig runs straight into box number six!

Too bad! No one wins the prize of a  !

bell, *carrot,*
guinea pig, *cage,*
block, *hoop*

Sitting outside her caravan, a fortune teller with

a  on her head and a gold

calls an invitation to Celeste and the Old Lady.

"Come in, and I will tell your fortune."

Inside, the lioness asks Celeste to pick out

one  , but Celeste can't decide which

to take. While she hesitates, the Old Lady asks,

"In your 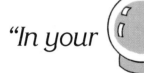 , is there anything for me?"

The fortune teller concentrates a moment, waving

her  . Then she announces to the

Old Lady: "I see...happiness, and a crown."

scarf,
earring,
card,
crystal ball,
fan

Who is that climbing the  ? A clown!

Everyone moves toward him as he cries, "Look

out! I'm about to fall down into the  !"

All the spectators are laughing, and one calls,

"You're losing your  !"

"Of course," says the clown, "because someone

has undone my  . If I catch him…"

More and more people gather. "Why do you have

that big bar of  ?" asks one child.

"To make the pole slippery!" answers the clown.

"Do you want to try climbing it?"

maypole,
pool,
pants,
suspenders,
soap

The game's object is to reach the  on

top of the pole. Poor Zephir isn't allowed to try.

It would be too easy for him. Pom gives him a

pink  as a consolation prize.

A hippopotamus tried first, but he quickly fell into

the water and lost his  !

"I'm going up now," says Rataxes loudly, handing

his yellow  to his wife. "I'll make it!"

But Rataxes is not a good climber—he's too heavy.

Reaching for the  , he loses his hold and

slides down into the pool!

wreath, cotton candy,
shoe, coat, bow

In leaving the pool, the drenched rhinoceros

king steps onto a nearby  . It spins

under his foot and gives him another fall!

Rataxes flattens a left by a spectator.

"Bravo, Arthur!" calls Zephir, hanging onto the

neck of a  to encourage his friend.

Arthur has finally climbed up to the wreath.

General Cornelius, with a big red in his

buttonhole, waits below to present the prize.

"Here is a  for the winner," declares

the general, giving the award to Arthur.

bottle,
hat,
giraffe,
flower,
medal

It's evening now, and everyone has gathered

around the  , where a buffet

is waiting. Babar congratulates the chef, who

blushes under his tall .

There is a huge ice sculpture of Babar, and Flora

has brought along a paper party  .

Arthur arrives as a hero and presents the maypole

wreath of flowers to the Old Lady.

"A for Arthur!" cries Zephir, who

is pretending to be the waiter. But he doesn't

forget to stop and pick up a  for himself.

table, chef's hat, lantern, sandwich, cookie

After dinner, in the ballroom, the children

watch the musicians tune their instruments.

"What is that long, curving gold one?" asks

Pom. "It's a  ," replies Arthur. "But I

think my favorite instrument of all is the  ."

One of the musicians begins to play a tune

on his  , which is Flora's favorite.

"Just like the song of the birds!" she exclaims.

"Look, there's a fine  ," says Alexander.

"I've always wanted to play one of those." Then

the ball begins with a tune from the  .

saxophone,
violin,
clarinet,
electric guitar,
accordion

Night has fallen, and high up in the sky is a

bright new crescent shining on the park.

"Look!" cries Zephir. "It's just like a big !"

The fireworks have started–how exciting!

Flora is delighted. Perched on Babar's shoulder,

she is pushing his  over one eye, so

that he can scarcely see a thing! The Old Lady

has on her to watch the splendid

display. Pom and Alexander have already climbed

onto the park  for a better view.

What a wonderful ending to a wonderful day!

moon, shooting star, crown, binoculars, fountain